Lucy and the Dragonfly

BY

LUCIE PAPINEAU

AND

CAROLINE HAMEL

AUZOU

There once was a little girl named Lucy.
Lucy lived on a blue planet that hung like a balloon in an immense universe;
on a continent so big it was hard to imagine;
in a country filled with lakes and forests, and sometimes snow;
in a village, at the end of a lane.
Yes, right there, in the pretty yellow house on the hill.

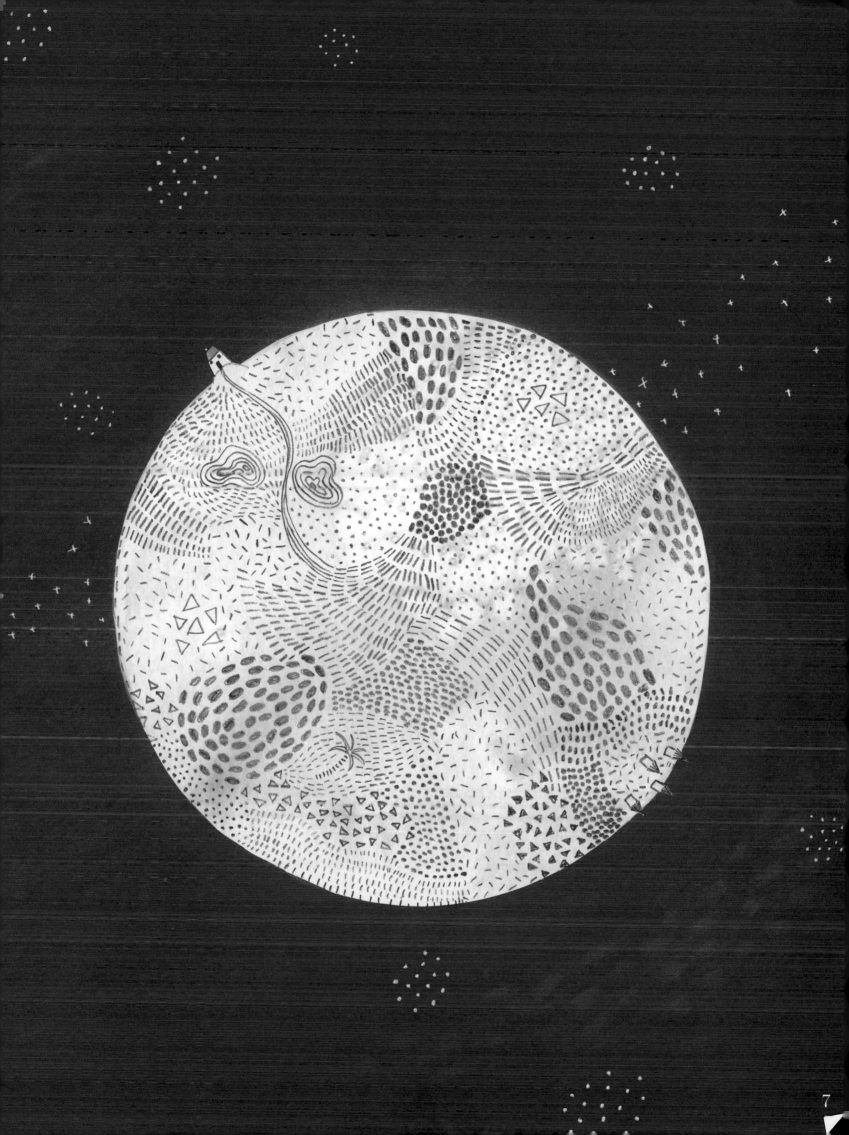

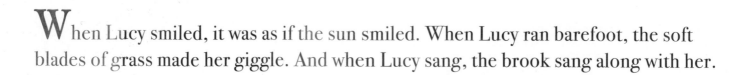

When Lucy smiled, it was as if the sun smiled. When Lucy ran barefoot, the soft blades of grass made her giggle. And when Lucy sang, the brook sang along with her.

A dragonfly often sat on Lucy's shoulder. She could see through her friend's fragile wings, and loved their soft touch on her cheeks.

"You're tickling me," whispered the little girl, laughing softly.

Lucy loved the dance of the seasons.

In the winter, she would make angels in the snow, and catch the star-shaped flakes on the tip of her tongue.

In the spring, her rosy cheeks bloomed like the flowers she loved so much.

In the summer, she would visit with the frogs in the brook, her hair blowing in the wind.

And when fall came, she heard the birds sing their good-byes as they flew off to their winter homes. Lucy liked to think that a tiny fairy had painted a thousand colors on the leaves of the tall trees.

Lucy could feel the Earth's heart beating, inside her heart.

But the whispering wind also told her all the bad things that humans were doing to their planet. The messages came from every corner of the Earth.

When dark spots covered the leaves on the tall trees and they fell before they could change color, Lucy's heart sank.

The blades of grass no longer made her giggle. They had yellowed, and died during a summer with too much heat, and no rain.

Even the brook no longer sang. Its water, once as clear as glass, was now muddy, and the frogs had disappeared.

Lucy no longer ran in the fields or played in the brook.

The little girl stopped coming outside. Instead, she stood looking through the window at the sky, dreaming of winter when the snow would return. But the snow never came, and the winter was no longer white and cold.

One morning, Lucy simply stopped looking at the sky.

The little girl had given up on the Earth. But before closing her window and shutting the curtains, Lucy breathed on the wings of her friend, the dragonfly.

"Go, fly to the brook," she said to her. "Go to sleep for the winter, which might still arrive . . ."

With a soft flutter, the dragonfly caressed Lucy's cheeks, and felt her tears. She caught them on her wings. Then she flew away.

That's when a tiny miracle began to unfold . . .

Lucy's tears fell from the dragonfly's wings as it flew above the brook. They shone on the dirty water, as if they were tiny reflections of the sun. Lucy's tears became messages launched out into the universe.

In those tears, was the story of the little girl who used to smile like the face of the sun. And her story made its way around the blue planet.

Her tears traveled from the brook to the river, from one river to the next, until the water reached the ocean. Finally, the story of Lucy came to the ears of a little boy named Tama. A boy who knew how to listen to the whispers in the wind, and the songs of the brook.

Tama ran until he reached the village. He knew that in the arms of his grandfather, he could say anything. Grandfather listened to the secrets that had fallen from the wings of the dragonfly. Stories that had been carried by the water, and whispered by the wind. Grandmother listened too.

They hurried to tell the village elders.

The elders had already noticed that the Earth's heartbeat had become weak.
Now they understood that to save this little girl, it would be necessary to
heal the Earth. But how? Their village was so tiny, and the planet was huge.

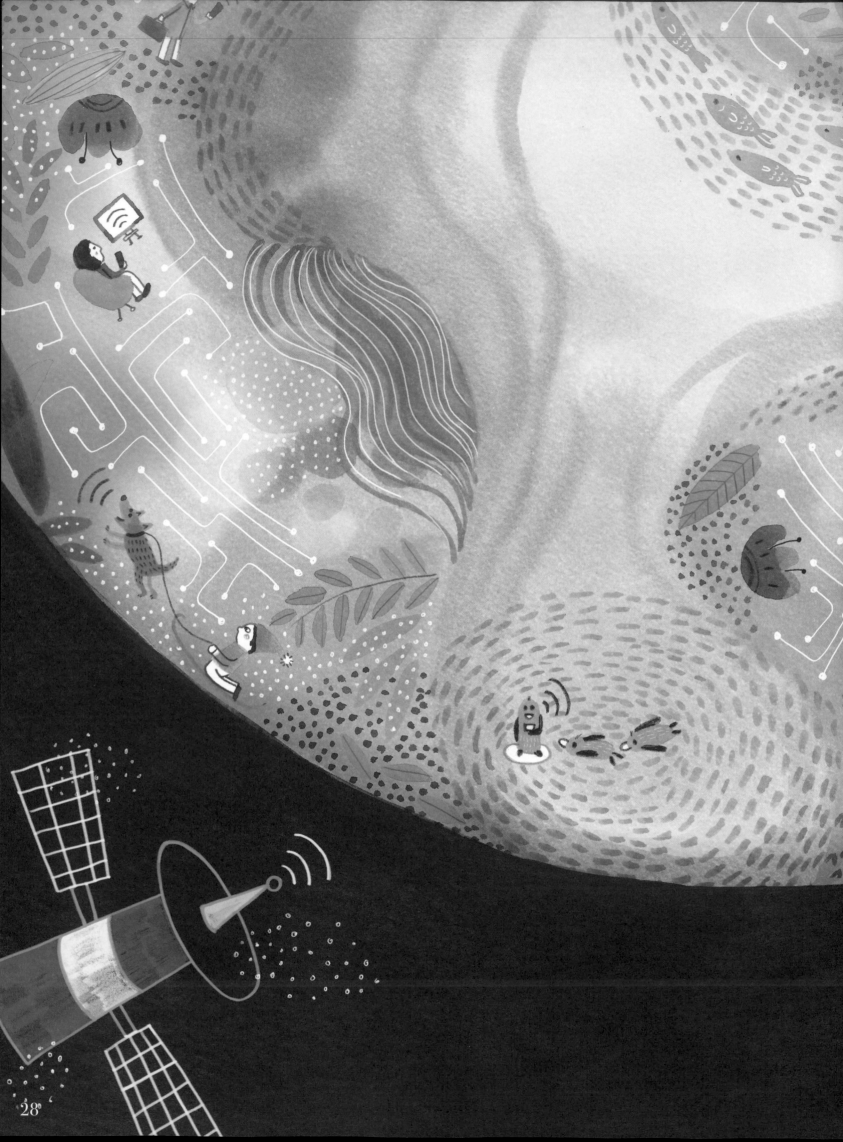

Tama jumped on his bike, and pedaled and pedaled, until he reached his cousin's house, the one with a phone.

Call after call carried the story of Lucy around the blue planet once more. It was spread by phones and tablets, computers and televisions. They all told the story of the little girl who had given up on the Earth. The little girl who had once smiled like the face of the sun.

All over the Earth, people wanted to cure this child, so they began to heal the sick planet. Some people did small things, others did big things, but together it all became one, enormous thing.

Spring finally came, and the sun shone once more. A little pink returned to Lucy's cheeks. One morning, she went out on her porch to wave to the birds returning from their long journey. Lucy listened to the brook which, after a heavy rain, was singing its song once more.

Of course, it was impossible to heal the blue planet in a single season. But Lucy was feeling better. She'd found what she needed . . .

HOPE.